Marilyn
Essertier

The Little Swiss Wood-Carver

THE LITTLE SWISS WOOD-CARVER

The LITTLE SWISS WOOD-CARVER

BY
MADELINE BRANDEIS

Producer of the Motion Pictures

"The Little Indian Weaver"
"The Wee Scotch Piper"
"The Little Dutch Tulip Girl"
"The Little Swiss Wood-Carver"

Distributed by the Pathé Exchange, Inc., New York City

Photographic Illustrations Made in Switzerland by the Author

GROSSET & DUNLAP
PUBLISHERS   NEW YORK
by arrangement with the A. Flanagan Company

FOREWORD

When this story is published, it will have been only a few weeks since my return from Europe whither I journeyed with Marie and Ref. Marie is my very little daughter and Ref is my very big reflex camera—both indispensable to the writing of this and of my future books about children of many lands.

Marie is eight and it was she who guided my footsteps along the right road towards child understanding, while the trusty camera made possible these illustrations. And the real reason for this foreword is not to praise my helpmates (though without them I should indeed have been helpless), but to explain that everything in these stories is for and about the modern child.

So many stories have been written bringing to you the lives of little Dutch Peter— little French Paul—and little frosty Eskimo —that I do not claim originality. But

Foreword

most books that Marie and I have read about foreign children were written many years ago and we wanted to see what was going on in European child life to-day. So we decided to take our eyes, ears and Ref across the ocean, and these books will show and tell you what we saw and heard.

We think Scotch Ian, Swiss Seppi, Dutch Katrina and the rest are really a lot like us after all, and what happened to them might easily happen to any of you. At least Marie thinks so, and I think Marie knows everything!

So, though I sign myself

Madeline Brandeis

I am really only

Marie's Mother.

To every child of every land,
  Little sister, little brother,
As in this book your lives unfold,
  May you learn to love each other.

CONTENTS

SEPPI'S CABIN UNDER THE MIGHTY WETTERHORN

The Little Swiss Wood-Carver

CHAPTER I

TO BE SWISS

Seppi was a little Swiss boy. But that does not explain Seppi, for there are many ways of being Swiss.

Suppose I said, "Mary is an American girl."

You would know, first, that she speaks English. Then you would be certain that she dresses in the same manner as other American girls do.

You would be sure that the flag flying from her window on the Fourth of July is the Stars and Stripes, no matter in what part of the United

States she lives. But with Swiss children, it is not like this at all.

Seppi, who lived in the Bernese Oberland, spoke German. The little Swiss children living in Geneva speak French. Down in the south of Switzerland in Locarno, they speak Italian.

Had Seppi taken a trip to Geneva or Locarno, he could not have understood the children there at all. Yet they are Swiss children, like Seppi.

This is because Switzerland is divided into twenty-two cantons, or states, as we would, no doubt, call them. Each canton has not only a different language but different customs and modes of dress, and a different cantonal flag.

COSTUMES OF CANTON APENZELL

Over them all, however, flies the Swiss flag, with its red ground and white cross. This is the emblem adopted years ago after a battle in which many lives were lost.

The red ground represents the

blood spilled on the battlefield. The white cross is in memory of the slain.

This beautiful flag is loved and honored by its people. Though they are divided into little sections, all so different, they are united and in sympathy with one another.

Just think of what a difference exists in each part of this little country! In the canton Vaud (vo), one finds a farming country. Here the people are engaged in tending their fat cattle and in raising grapes in their excellent vineyards.

Their language is French. Their costumes, which are worn only on special occasions, are of a picturesque green and white. The women wear large hats, with grapes hanging from the brim. The men are dressed in velvet trousers, with little straw caps perched on one side of the head.

If you should travel to the Bernese Oberland, you would find yourself among German-speaking people. This section is among the mountains in canton Bern. Among these mountains you would see snowcapped peaks, little wooden cabins, and many goats.

On fair days, you would see costumes entirely different from what you saw below in sunny canton Vaud.

Here, then, in the midst of goats, mountains, and cabins, lived this little boy, Seppi. I shall tell you about him. You know that he spoke German.

SEPPI'S CABIN UNDER THE MIGHTY WETTERHORN

His father was a Swiss wood-carver. Wood-carving is an interesting occupation, and is done in this particular canton of Switzerland.

The Swiss are a hard-working people. They have to work hard, because their tiny country is entirely hemmed in by other countries and has no seaport. So there is hardly enough food to feed the people.

Although the great mountains, the Alps, are full of minerals, it would be too great an expense to dig them out.

So we find this little country with everything to make it poor. But instead of suffering, want, and starvation, we find here one of the most prosperous and important countries of Europe. This condition is due only to the industrious Swiss people themselves.

Have you ever wondered where those pretty little music-boxes, which play so sweetly, are made? If you look inside, you will find the words, "Made in Switzerland."

Then, who does not want to own a Swiss-made watch? For everyone knows that they are among the best in the world.

When you stop to buy a bar of chocolate, look on the wrapper and you will, doubtless, see the words, "Imported from Switzerland."

Many packages of cheese, sold at our markets, are imported from Swit-

SEPPI WAS A GOAT-BOY

zerland. They are, perhaps, made in the very mountains where Seppi lived.

It is possible that you have eaten some of the cheese made from the milk of the Bernese cows, which roam those beautiful mountains. But they do not climb so high as Seppi did. You see, Seppi was a goat-boy and goats always go higher than cows.

Seppi perched all day long on the mountain side and watched his goats. Below, his father sat outside their tiny wooden cabin. The father was busy carving.

Wood-carving is another of Switzerland's many industries. The different things made by wood-carvers and sent to all parts of the world or sold to the tourists in the Swiss cities are too numerous to mention.

Of course you have seen the cuckoo clocks. You have doubtless heard the saucy little bird that pops his head out of the window every hour and chirps, "Cuckoo, cuckoo!" These fanciful clocks are made in Switzerland and carved by the wood-carvers.

All kinds of novelties and children's toys are made by these same wood-carvers. Joseph, Seppi's father, was one of the cleverest.

He made his living by carving for the shops in the villages below. He sold his carvings for enough money to keep himself and his little son through the long winter months.

At this period, the tourists in Switzerland are few, and the shops buy little. It is only for a short season that these people gather their harvest. They depend upon the tourists to supply them with the greater part of their living.

Everyone wants to come to Switzerland and see the renowned mountains and the glorious lakes. Everyone is attracted by the many interesting sights to be seen in that fine land. So this is how many of the Swiss people make a living.

The country is dotted with the finest hotels, because, of course, the travelers must be made comfortable. Swiss hotels are known for their comfort

and delicious food. So you see, hotel-
keeping is yet another Swiss pro-
fession.

But think of the long months
when nobody comes! The people are
hemmed in by snow and ice. Then,
sometimes there is much suffering.
This happens if enough has not been
gathered in during harvest time.

Seppi, too, had known suffering. It
was before the boy could remember,
that he and his father had lived alone
on the mountain side. One carved,
and the other herded. Many a winter
found them cold and without enough
bread to eat.

It sometimes seemed strange to
Seppi, when he thought of the snug

resorts so near. These resorts, in fact, lay almost at their feet. Here people had warmth and fine food and wine, while he and his old father often shivered and went hungry.

But you must not think that this was always the case. Very often Joseph would receive large orders for carvings from the shops below. Then he would carve all day and sing to himself. For he knew that Seppi and he would be comfortable during the winter.

Besides, in the shops they liked Joseph's work. All over Switzerland, his lovely carved animals were sold. Many had even journeyed to America. For Joseph was a true artist, and

"IF I COULD ONLY CARVE LIKE THAT!"

carved each piece with a sincere love of his subject.

He had always carved animals. He liked to carve the graceful chamois— the animal found only in Switzerland. The little goat, and Switzerland's own dog, the noble St. Bernard, were also Joseph's favorite subjects.

Often his work table looked like a small zoo. At those times, Seppi stood and gazed in rapture at the fine array of lifelike wooden figures displayed before him. For Seppi loved his father's work better than anything else in the world.

Sometimes, while the old man worked, the boy knelt by his side and watched. Then Seppi's eyes caressed the growing beauty under the master's knife. Meanwhile, with each chip of Joseph's knife, the figure would take on a lifelike look.

Seppi often sighed, "Ah, Father, if I could only carve like that!"

But Joseph only shook his head, covered with its black silk cap and tassel.

He replied, "No, Seppi, my son. You are too young to carve, and I have no money to send you to school to learn. You must tend the goats."

Then Seppi smiled sadly at the lovely work, which he so longed to do. With a deep sigh, he gathered his goats together and wended his way toward the high places.

CHAPTER II

SEPPI

"Seppi" may seem a strange name for a boy. But in Switzerland it is a very common name. Seppi's real name was Joseph, like his father's. He was called Seppi, just as you would be called Billy, if you were named William after your father.

Up the mountain each morning went Seppi. But first he ate his portion of brown bread and cheese, as he and his father sat outside their cabin on a little wooden bench. Meanwhile, the coffee boiled on a rough stove beside them.

THE MORNING MEAL

One spring morning, Seppi said to his father, "What a fine day, Father!"

He stretched his strong young arms and looked below at the rolling hills. In among them, their dots of villages nestled like bright little flowers.

Ringlets of clouds surrounded the mountain peaks above. These clouds made circles like those made by cigarette-smokers to amuse children.

The lofty Wetterhorn, the highest mountain in Switzerland, poked its head over the top as though to say, "You may circle and circle the sky, but you can never cover me!"

The Jungfrau (yoong'frou), one of the most beautiful of Switzerland's mountains, looked across at the haughty Wetterhorn. Then she shyly covered her graceful, snow-white head in a fleecy cloud.

"The top of the Jungfrau looks so close to-day! I should like to climb up there," said Seppi, longingly.

Like all the Swiss, Seppi was a climber. Sometimes he would try to rival his spry companions, the goats, in clambering high up the mountain. He went so high that he could look down and see even his own mountain cabin as a speck below.

But he had little time for these pleasures. In fact he was kept to his post most of the day. The goats were his charges, and he was paid, though ever so little, to take them to pasture each day.

There were perhaps a hundred goats — thin black creatures, with kindly, intelligent faces. They belonged to neighboring peasants. Their owners had no time to climb with

them while they grazed, and so engaged a goat-boy to do this work.

Seppi would take them to an alp,
which is not a mountain, as so many
children think. To be sure, the chain
of mountains is called "The Alps."
But in reality, an alp is a little fertile
meadow, nestled on the side of the
rocky mountains.

Here, where the grass is long and
sweet, Seppi took his goats each day.
When this source was exhausted, they
went to another alp.

An alp is like an oasis in a desert—a
fertile spot. Around it, all is barren
and bleak. From the valleys below
the alps, patches of green, are clearly
seen upon the mountain sides. There

are little snowy blotches around them, which seem not to belong there at all.

But without these green mountain meadows, the goat owners would be in trouble. They would not know how to feed their animals.

On this bright day, the curly clouds were teasing the tall mountain tops. The roofs of the houses glistened below in the sunshine. Seppi's heart was light as he said good-bye to his father and went about his duty.

His father, finishing the morning meal, proudly watched the tall, straight boy. Seppi slung the curved horn about his shoulders and started up the mountain side. He blew a blast as he stopped at each goat barn.

At the sound, the goats came out. Gradually the whole herd was gathered together in a happy band, as they frisked up to their alp.

It might truly be called their tableland, as high flat land is called. It was indeed the goats' breakfast, lunch, and dinner table. So it was no wonder that they hurried along so fast that Seppi did not have to urge them.

Joseph watched the goat-boy out of sight. Then he turned slowly toward the stove. Here he gathered up the remains of the breakfast and prepared to wash the dishes at the long, wooden trough.

Joseph was not in a hurry to-day, so his fingers moved slowly. His

THE DAY'S WORK IS OVER

thoughts were dreary. For he knew
that when this little work was over,
he would have no more to do that day.

It was late spring now, and the orders were not coming from the villages. The winter had been long and

hard. There had been many nights of cold blasts, when the house had trembled. When morning came, the snow outside had hemmed them in.

Another winter like that would be too terrible to imagine. Work must come to the poor wood-carver this summer, or he feared for his life and that of his son.

To be sure, there were many of Joseph's carvings laid out on the table. For the old man had not been idle through the winter months. Though he had not been ordered to work, he had prepared animals of all descriptions.

For he had hoped that summer would bring tourists to the villages.

He had hoped that the tourists would bring money to the shops. Then the shops would send orders to him.

But spring was wearing on, and the shops had not asked Joseph for carvings. Seppi had gone below several times, but he always returned at night without orders for his father.

No work! Joseph was dreading his days alone there with his wintry thoughts. They tormented him even in the midst of the pleasant, balmy springtime.

But Seppi, on his mountain, was not unhappy. He was young and easily forgot the pain of past hardships.

Sometimes he felt sorry that he could not carve. Still, the little goat-boy could only dream that some day he might learn to carve like his gifted father. Just how he would learn, however, he could not guess.

On the mountain side, he had often taken bits of wood and, with his crude pocket-knife, tried to imitate Joseph's animals. Behind a rock was, in fact, Seppi's own workshop.

Here might be seen samples of his work, which he had kept for many months. There were lopsided wooden goats and earless cats. There were many-legged bears, and a chamois with a camel's hump.

But along the row, farther on, was another cat, which had ears. Also, the second chamois' hump had disappeared, and he resembled a real chamois. All of which showed that little Seppi was improving.

Though he carved, he did not tell his father. Joseph's work was perfect. Seppi felt that he could never show his poor attempts to the great master.

But to-day Seppi was not carving. He was longing to climb to the top of the Jungfrau. Not many people have accomplished this feat.

The boy was gazing at the mountain in silent admiration. It was indeed a lovely white Jungfrau, a word that in German means "young lady."

Seppi's eyes were sharp, and he could see far off. As he looked, he saw something moving. The figure was very high up the mountain indeed. He had never before seen a figure up there.

The boy was at once interested. Standing up, he shaded his eyes, the better to see ahead. Yes. There was something alive up there. As he strained his eyes, he saw that there must be several people climbing the Jungfrau.

Seppi's first thought was not of danger, but of admiration and a little envy. These were, no doubt, holiday-makers. For the first thing a Swiss will do, when he is given a day of rest, is to climb the mountains.

It did not seem at all strange to little Swiss Seppi, who wished that he

HE SHADED HIS EYES AND LOOKED

might be with them. All day long, he watched the climbers. Though they did not reach the top, they went very high.

As they descended, the boy began to wonder about them. He was quite sure that they were Swiss men.

Doubtless they had tried to gain the thrill of thrills and mount to the summit. Failing, they had probably turned back. He pictured to himself the rugged Alpine men, with alpenstock and bags slung upon their backs, and heavy-nailed shoes.

The people drew nearer. Seppi stood and craned his neck for a closer glimpse. Yes. They were going to pass him, and he could see them at close range. But was it possible? Seppi rubbed his eyes. Yes. It was as he had thought.

At the head of the party walked a woman!

Seppi's eyes grew big with amazement. Then he smiled a broad smile, while a look of admiration came into his face. Thus the lady came upon him. She returned his smile.

"Good day," she said in English.

Seppi shook his head. "I do not understand," he answered in German.

By this time, the rest of the party, two men, had come up. Seppi observed immediately that they were English or American tourists.

"You have watched our descent?"

asked the lady in perfect German. She still smiled at the goat-boy.

"Yes," answered he warmly. "And a fine climb you made! I have been watching you all the day."

"You did not know that a lady was up there?" she smiled.

"Ah, no," answered Seppi. "It was truly a great surprise."

The lady spoke in English to the two gentlemen. Then the three seated themselves wearily beside Seppi.

"Is it far to Grindelwald?" asked the lady, in German, to Seppi.

"Yes, very far," he replied. "A three hours' walk. But that could not be far to you, who are so great a climber."

A twinkle came into his eyes.

The lady laughed. "But now we have had enough for the day," she said. "We are tired."

Seppi wondered whether he dared suggest his little house as a haven of rest.

While he was pondering, one of the gentlemen asked, "Do you live near by?"

Seppi answered, "It is a walk of an hour below to my home. You are welcome to stay the night."

It was said simply yet sincerely. For the Swiss are an honest people and offer what they have, because they like to help people.

Besides, they are always courteous and hospitable.

Even in the schoolroom, Swiss children are taught to be courteous to strangers.

"Remember that the stranger is the friend of Switzerland. It is through the tourist that we make our bread!" So ran his earliest lesson.

So the invitation was offered cordially and from the heart, though Seppi knew that in the rude hut there was little comfort. At the same time, he knew that if the strangers accepted his invitation, he would have to sleep in the goat-barn or on the porch floor.

Still he hoped that they would come. He could see that they were tired, especially the lady. So he wanted to make them comfortable.

"I can run down and have my father prepare supper," he said.

But the lady put a gentle hand on his sleeve.

Meanwhile the gentleman spoke, "No; thank you. We must get back. We are awaited in the village. But might we, perhaps, stop at your house to rest and drink a glass of cool water?"

"Ah, yes," said Seppi, jumping up.

Blowing on his horn, he soon had his goats gathered together. Then his new-found friends followed him down the mountain side.

CHAPTER III

AN ORDER AND A STORY

To the home of Joseph came the boy and the travelers. The old carver was indeed surprised to see his son bringing these strange people with him.

Seppi soon told his father of the daring exploit of the lady. He found she had come all the way from America with her husband and her brother, the other gentleman.

Joseph joined in his son's admiration of the foreign lady, who was called Mrs. Brownley.

She smiled at them and said, "But

GRAND ST. BERNARD HOSPICE

that is nothing. We have been all over Switzerland and climbed higher even than that."

Seppi was at once attentive and serious.

"Oh, it would be a wonderful thing,"

he said, "to go all over Switzerland and see its many beauties."

Mrs. Brownley lifted her brows in surprise.

"But you are Swiss, are you not?" she asked. "Have you never seen your own fair country?"

Seppi hung his head. "We are very poor," he said. "I have never been farther than the village below."

The lady became grave.

"That is indeed a misfortune!" she exclaimed. "To live in so lovely a country and to see nothing of it! But," she brightened, "you are very young. One day you will go. For I have heard that Swiss children are always sent away to other cantons. Thus they

may learn to speak the other lan-
guages of their country."

Joseph nodded and answered, "Yes;
that is true. I hope that my Seppi
will some day have that chance. For
he now speaks only one language and
that, for a Swiss, is not enough."

The three travelers drank the cool-
ing drink served them by Seppi and
rested on the little shaded porch of
the cabin. They said they had heard
of Joseph's work.

"Ah," said the lady. "There are so
many beautiful wood-carvings sold in
the shops throughout Switzerland. I
have seen and admired them. Do you
think I might see yours?"

Joseph took the strangers to the

side of the house, where he kept his work table. Here he had been finishing a little piece. He showed them some of his beautiful animals.

"How exquisite!" exclaimed Mrs. Brownley. "Oh, you are truly an artist! And would you be too busy to carve something special for me?"

Joseph could not answer for a moment. The thought of his being too busy, after his worry and sufferings, struck him as almost laughable.

"Ah, no, lady," he said. "I shall be glad to do a work for you."

There was feeling in Joseph's words. Here at last was an order. Here was some one who admired his work. The summer might yet bring

THE ST. BERNARD MOUNTAINS

money, and relief from fear of the coming winter.

"Then let me tell you what I should like," said Mrs. Brownley. "But first I must explain why I want it."

She then told Joseph and his son how, on a day not so long ago, she had gone to visit the famous old St. Bernard Hospice.

This hospice is at the top of the St. Bernard mountains. It was founded by the great Father Bernard many, many years ago. Here dwelt the Father and his priests.

Through the long, snowy winter months, they watched and searched for those who had lost their way in the snow.

Father Bernard began raising a new breed of dogs. They are now known as St. Bernard—the big, shaggy, wrinkled-faced dogs! It was here, high up in the mountains, at this hospice, that these animals were first bred.

The dogs were trained by Father Bernard to go out into the snow and bring home wanderers. Some of these unfortunates fell and were liable to be frozen in the snow.

But with a little barrel of whisky and a packet of chocolate about their necks, these fine animals saved many a life.

By their keen sense of smell they would always lead the lost one to the hospice. Here he would be assured of a warm meal and a bed for the night.

"I visited the hospice," said Mrs. Brownley, "and I saw some of these dogs. I loved them at once. We spent the night at the hospice, where a stranger can still find refuge without charge.

"Early the next morning before daylight, I got up. For I was anxious to explore the mountains. Alone I wandered about.

"I enjoyed the fresh mountain air made crisp by the clumps of snow which, though spring was there, were still thick about.

"Not realizing it, I wandered afar. Before I knew it, I was lost. I tried to find my way back, but in vain. True,

ONE OF THE PRIESTS AND SOME OF THE
GREAT ST. BERNARD DOGS

we had motored up on a bus along a
modern mountain highway.

"But the wildness there in the
heart of the mountains made it seem
years and years ago, before the time
of the automobile.

"All that morning I wandered, until it seemed that it was late noon.

"Hungry and tired, I sat down and waited. I could not think what my husband would do. I knew he must be frightfully worried. I was at the point of tears myself.

"I was about to begin calling again, as I had been doing for several hours. Then I heard a sound, as of soft, padded footsteps, coming toward me. Nearer and nearer it came, and then the sniff-sniff of an animal. I was, by this time, very tired and frightened, and I let out a scream.

"But upon recovering my senses, I saw a surprising sight.

"I saw, not a wild beast as I had

MRS. BROWNLEY'S FRIEND

imagined, but a fine big dog standing before me!

" 'A St. Bernard!' I cried, and threw my arms about the big animal's shaggy neck.

"He was panting and hot, and had

evidently been sent to search for me. It seemed to me he smiled and beckoned me with his fine eyes to follow him. It is needless for me to tell you that I was brought back to the hospice in safety by my guide.

"And that is why I am going to ask you, Mr. Wood-Carver, to make me a copy of that dog. I want to have a remembrance of my friend before me always."

CHAPTER IV

JOSEPH CARVES

Days of carving! Happily Joseph worked at his task, which greatly pleased him. While working on the wooden dog, he often thought of the American lady's story. On this account, he put feeling and love into his work.

Then, too, Joseph's mind was at rest. The lady had not only admired his work and ordered this dog. She had also bought many of Joseph's other carvings. It was a happy time for the old man and his son.

The son watched his father's fingers

JOSEPH CARVES THE LADY'S DOG

as they deftly cut the splinters of wood. How skillfully they carved an image lifelike and fine! The boy longed more than ever to carve like this himself.

Poor little goat-boy! Each day,

after the goats were settled on the alp, he took out his pocket-knife and carved.

At night when he returned, he took his work from his little side pouch and stole up to the work table. Then while Joseph was away at some other task, he compared it with the work of his father.

For a great resolution had sprung up in Seppi's breast. He, too, would carve. He had a real affection for the fine St. Bernard dog which had saved the lady. This love inspired him so much that he vowed to copy his father's carving.

Joseph had no idea of Seppi's plan. He sometimes wondered why the boy, who was usually so prompt at meal-time, was late. When the soup was ready, Joseph often had to call his son to come.

When the call came, Seppi was usually comparing with critical eye his latest work on the wooden dog with the work of his father. Hearing the call, he hurriedly replaced his carving in his pouch, put his father's back on the table, and hastened to his dinner.

"Soon the carving will be ready, Seppi," said Joseph one evening. "And then you shall take it to Mrs. Brownley at the hotel in Grindelwald."

"Yes, father," smiled Seppi. "And how pleased she will be! For it is a beautiful carving."

Then the young carver looked wistfully at his pouch hanging by his side. While Joseph turned to cut the big loaf of bread, Seppi silently took out his precious work and looked at it once more.

Before his father turned around, Seppi's carving was back in his pouch. The old man watched the hungry boy devouring his bread and cheese. And all the time, he never suspected that so near him was a model of his own work.

As Seppi compared his little dog with his father's, he smiled a happy, satisfied smile. Though he dared not even think it, in his heart he felt that it was almost as good as Joseph's.

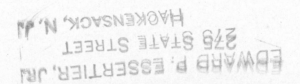

So the time came when Joseph's work was finished. Early one morning, Seppi donned his best clothes, the ancient costume of canton Bern. It consisted of velvet pants, a little velvet jacket with puffy sleeves and gold braid, and a small, round cap of the same material.

It was an important occasion to these simple peasants when Seppi went to the village. And now, of all times, he was to deliver the precious dog to the kind lady. He looked forward with pleasure to seeing her once more.

On Seppi's back Joseph strapped the basket, which is used throughout Switzerland. Peasants, tradespeople,

"GUARD THE CARVING, SEPPI!"

and children use it to carry all manner of articles, from fish to soap.

Into the basket Joseph put his son's lunch. It was made up of sandwiches, done up in a clean red and white kerchief.

Then the carver held up his work— the lovely dog. It was stained and polished and appeared so natural that to look into its eyes was to look into those of the animal itself.

"Guard the carving, Seppi," said Joseph. "Remember that the money it brings will buy food for many days."

So saying, he wrapped another print kerchief about the figure and laid it gently into the basket.

Seppi placed his two hands lovingly upon his father's shoulders. He took his leave, assuring Joseph that he would guard the precious carving with care.

Now, although Joseph was poor, he was well known about the country-side. Many of the people believed that because he was such a fine artist, he was equally successful and rich. They knew or thought that his works sold for much money.

So they did, when he was fortunate enough to sell them. But that was not often and, as you have heard, often the carver and his son went hungry, in spite of his fame.

That day two boys followed Seppi

as he wended his way down the mountain paths. As he went through the grottos and alongside the trickling streams and gushing waterfalls, those two boys behind him laid their plans.

They knew that Seppi was going to sell his father's carving. They had heard that Joseph's work brought large sums of money. It is strange sometimes how news flies about.

Throughout those mountains, the peasants had heard the news of Joseph's order from the American lady. Around many a simple board, they had talked about the carver and his work.

They had wondered how much money he would receive from the

TWO BOYS WATCHED SEPPI

lady. To most of these people the news was pleasant. They rejoiced that the carver was favored by fortune.

But among those who heard the talk and wondered about the amount the

carving would bring, were the two
boys who followed Seppi. These boys
did not rejoice in the carver's good
fortune. On the other hand, they
longed to have the money for themselves.

They were bad boys, who had been
led into evil ways. They had never
had parents to love and teach them.
They had lived with a peasant, working for him as farm hands.

Dissatisfied with their lot, they had
planned for many months to escape.
They wanted to run away, but the
problem of having no money had
bothered them.

They had heard this talk of Joseph's
good luck and the money which Seppi

would collect from the tourist below. As a result, a wicked plan had entered their minds. So these two boys followed little Seppi that day.

On and on went the happy lad. His outstretched arms caressing the very air of his beloved land. He was a true Swiss peasant, whose blessing was his country, and his country his first love.

The little birds sang in the trees. As he went lower, the ginger-colored cows, grazing contentedly, posed for him to admire them.

At last, hot and ready for a rest, Seppi stopped in the shadow of a shrine. It was a tall cross upon which was a carving of the Virgin, decorated with spring flowers. The flowers were

COMPARING THE CARVINGS

doubtless some peasant's offering. Throwing himself down, the boy slung the basket from off his back. He lay for a moment on the soft ground. Then, sitting up, he took his father's treasure, the carving, from the basket. He wanted to look once more at its beauty. Young artist that he was, he thrilled as he held up the carved dog and studied its graceful lines, its beauty.

All the while, the two boys slid noiselessly behind a tree and watched.

"That is the carving," whispered one to the other. "It is very fine. It will bring much money."

The other nudged his brother impatiently

"Come then. Do not stand and gape at it," he said, "but let us take it quickly and run."

As he spoke, Seppi took from his pocket his own carving and started to compare the two.

WHILE SEPPI PRAYED

"It is the last time you will be together," he said wistfully to the two
little works in his hands. Then, cock-
ing his head on one side as he had
often seen his father do when regard-
ing with critical eye, he smiled.

Half aloud and half to himself, with a tremble in his voice, he said, "Ah, little dog of mine, I do believe you are well made!"

Sighing, he replaced the two pieces of carving, one in his pouch, the other in the basket. He carefully wrapped his father's carving in the kerchief. Then, rising, he went to the cross.

Doffing his hat, the boy knelt. A silent prayer came from his lips—a prayer of joy in life, of gratitude, of youth and springtime!

CHAPTER V

As Seppi prayed, the boys sidled, like two gliding snakes, from behind the tree. Stealthily and swiftly they crouched until they were upon Seppi's basket.

The lad prayed, knowing little of the danger at his back. He was content to be at peace and to kneel in silent prayer.

At last he rose slowly, his soft brown eyes lifted in devout admiration to the face of the Virgin. Then he turned.

At first Seppi thought the basket

SEPPI LOOKED FOR HIS BASKET

had rolled down the little hill. Still, that could hardly have been. He could see below, about and above. The basket was not where he had left it, nor was it anywhere about.

Passing his hand slowly across his brow, the boy turned again. Below, far below, along the pathway, ran the two boys fast, fast. The basket—Seppi's basket—was dangling between them. Their feet were flying and their arms were waving.

Gone! The little dog—his father's! The lady's! Oh, wicked, heartless boys!

What could poor Seppi do? Return to his father? Never! Poor Joseph, who had struggled so through the past hard winter! Those frightful nights all came back to Seppi now, as he stood on that hill.

He seemed to stand on the top of a cloud, while the whole world spun around below him. Joseph was counting on the money for the dog. It would almost bring them through the snowy winter months.

Seppi felt he could not return and tell his father that the little work was gone—stolen. It would break the old man's heart. And Mrs. Brownley was waiting, too. Poor little goat-boy Seppi! He stood before the shrine. His hand felt for his own little dog— the copy of his father's work. It was lying safe in his pouch.

At Grindelwald there are many lovely hotels. Mr. and Mrs. Brownley were stopping at one of them. It had a spacious garden lawn, with bright-colored tables and chairs. From this spot, one could overlook the valley below and gaze in awe at the stately mountain peaks above.

Mrs. Brownley had been long in Switzerland. It was only because her husband insisted that she was now preparing to leave what she called her fairyland.

Mr. Brownley had a large store in America. He sometimes told his wife that, if he did not go back to work, she would never be able to come to Switzerland again. Nor could he buy her the fine things she loved so well.

For Mrs. Brownley had bought a little of everything which the busy little country had to offer. This day, she sat out in the garden. Spread out before her were the many treasures she had gathered throughout her journeys to all parts of Switzerland.

Mrs. Brownley would not stay indoors, even to pack her belongings.

"I must see the mountains as much as I can, now that you are taking me from them so soon," she told her husband.

He smiled, as he watched her with a huge crate before her.

She wrapped each little souvenir tenderly and placed each trinket and novelty with care inside the box.

"I cannot think why the wood-carver in the mountains never sent the carving I ordered," she said seriously to her husband, as she packed. "To-morrow we are leaving, and the boy has not yet brought it. I did so want that St. Bernard dog to take home with me. I felt that the old carver was truly the one to make it for me."

"No doubt the order was too small," answered her husband. "They tell me in the shops that old Joseph is considered a master. He evidently receives large orders from them. He was probably too busy to complete your little work."

Mrs. Brownley did not reply, but there was keen disappointment in her face. She had taken a fancy to Seppi, and she had set her heart on having the dog. To leave Switzerland without it and without seeing the boy again would be hard.

Besides, she was surprised that Seppi and his father did not keep their word. She had trusted them.

Into the big, bright garden Seppi advanced hesitatingly. Then he saw his friend, the American lady, standing at a table overlooking the deep valley below.

His hand was clutching his carving, still inside the pouch. He had made a decision at the shrine. Now, with a

INTO THE GARDEN CAME SEPPI

silent prayer in his heart, he had come to sell the only carving he had to sell —his own.

Would she guess? To him the little work had seemed good, when he had compared it with his father's. But as the boy thought it over, he was afraid and trembled. How bold he was to suppose that he could carve as well as Joseph! Very slowly poor Seppi approached his friend, Mrs. Brownley. She looked up and saw him.

"Ah, Seppi, it is you!" she called. "Come. I have been waiting for you."

Seppi approached the table. For the first time, he saw the lovely Swiss work spread out on it. Then the bashful goat-boy, remembering what he carried in his pouch, grew afraid.

"You look at my treasures, Seppi," said the lady pleasantly. "I have collected them from all over your beautiful Switzerland. Shall I tell you about them?"

"Ah, yes," breathed the relieved boy.

His mission would be put off for at least a short time. Besides, he did so want to hear of the lady's travels.

Lifting a toy Swiss mountain house with a clock in the center, Mrs. Brownley said, "This lovely little clock was made in La Chaux-de-Fonds (la-sho'-de-fon'), a city of watch factories. There every other building is a watch or clock works. When I went there, I visited three of them.

"The Swiss watches are known all over the world. It was a great privilege to me to see them being made. La Chaux-de-Fonds is in the canton Neufchatel (nu-sha-tel')."

THE TRAVELER SHOWS THE BOY HER TREASURES

Putting down the clock, she reached for a music box. As she touched a button, the little box began to play. Strains of grand opera were wafted through the air. Each tune was in perfect harmony, with not a beat missing, coming in soft, melodious tones.

To Seppi, it seemed too beautiful to be true. The lady turned the little box, with its cover showing a painted Alpine scene, over in her hand.

Then she said, "In St. Croix (kroi), canton Vaud (vo), the music boxes are made. This is the only city in the world where they hold a certain secret used in the manufacture of these novelties. It was therefore difficult for strangers to go through the factories. They guard their secret jealously and fear spies.

"But we were fortunate in seeing a factory. We were amazed to find that it takes thirty-seven people to make one little movement. The factory itself is small, as the detailed parts are done by people in their homes.

"Every part is made by hand and by a specialist. Then the whole set of works is fitted together and put into the box at the factory.

"Thousands and thousands of tunes are used. As soon as a new popular one comes out, it is put into a music box. Italian tunes are sent to Italy, French tunes to France, American tunes to America, and so forth.

"Lovely wooden trays which play music when lifted, are also made here. Other articles made are powder boxes, which play lively melodies when the covers are removed. There are many other musical novelties. One of the jolliest is the Christmas tree base, which turns the tree about to the tune of tinkling music."

Seppi was spellbound. At Mrs. Brownley's suggestion, he lifted from the table a fruit dish.

She said, "Listen."

It began to play a Swiss air.

"You know that," said Mrs. Brownley, as Seppi's face lit up.

Then she amused him by showing him various articles of wood-carving. Some of them were nutcrackers in the forms of funny-faced men, whose mouths opened wide to receive nuts.

Some were children's toys. Others were faces with eyes that rolled when

SCHOOL OF WOOD-CARVING AT BRIENZ

a string was pulled. Still others were graceful wood-carvings, which delighted Seppi.

"These I bought at the school for wood-carvers at Brienz (bre-ents')," said Mrs. Brownley. "You will surely be interested in that, for it is there that young lads are trained to be wood-carvers. I saw there twenty-five or thirty students, some specializing in decorative art, some in animal life, and others in human sculpture.

"All are taught, free of charge. But their works are kept by the school and sold. It takes many years to be proficient at this art."

"Ah, yes," said Seppi, "and I should like to go there some day."

"So you may, Seppi," answered the lady, smiling at him.

"No. I am afraid my father could never afford to send me away for so long," said Seppi. "I must tend the goats and bring to him what little I make. For sometimes the shops do not buy his work, and then there is no bread to eat."

Mrs. Brownley did not answer, but turned her head away. She was sorry for the boy and sorry, too, for the carver, whose art she truly admired.

As she tried to straighten some of her trinkets on the table, Seppi remembered his coming trial. His hand felt for his pouch and clutched it so tightly that the sharp corners of wood hurt his flesh.

His eyes roved over the table. He saw there the wood-carvings made by students of the school in Brienz. They were trained, clever boys—oh, they were so much cleverer than he!

A sudden chill overcame poor Seppi. He was afraid Mrs. Brownley would at this moment ask for his father's carving. For she had surely expected him to bring it. Like a drowning person clutching at a straw, he hoped to delay that moment.

He said, "Dear lady, would you tell me something of your travels through Switzerland? I have been nowhere. Please tell me what you have seen."

Mrs. Brownley nodded kindly and motioned him to a chair.

"Sit down, Seppi," she said, "and I will tell you."

CHAPTER VI
SWITZERLAND'S HISTORY

On Lake Leman, better known as the Lake of Geneva, stands the Castle of Chillon (shil′on). The famous poem, "The Prisoner of Chillon," by Lord Byron, was inspired by this old castle, with its sad history.

It is, without doubt, the most interesting historical monument in Switzerland. Within its walls have passed scenes of tragedy.

It contains torture-chambers, where witches and sorcerers were burned. How well could the deep waters that wash the banks moan the

THE CASTLE OF CHILLON

echo of sufferers who lived many cen-
turies ago!

The castle first belonged to the
bishops of Sion. "The Prisoner of
Chillon," Byron's poem, was written
around the incident of the imprison-

ment here of Francois Bonivard (fran-
swa' bo-ne-var') for six years.

Switzerland's hero, William Tell, is
a hero to more than the Swiss. William Tell is a name well known among
children throughout the world. The
picture of the great archer aiming at
the apple upon the head of his little
son is quite clear to every child.

In Altdorf, in canton Uri, stands a
massive statue—in the center of the
town. It shows William Tell, the stal-
wart peasant. His arm is about his
son's shoulders, and his head is raised
in defiance.

William Tell defied the great Aus-
trian governor, Gessler. At that
time, Austria dominated that part of

Switzerland. For at this period, Switzerland was not a free country, as it is to-day. The part in which William Tell lived was ruled by Austria.

The governor, Gessler, was arrogant, as well as cruel. He had raised a pole in the square of the little town of Altdorf.

On that pole he had put a hat—the black-plumed hat of the Duke of Austria! Everyone who passed through the square was obliged to salute and bow to the ducal headgear.

On a holiday—a time of joyous celebration—all the people were making merry in the little hamlet. Even the people from the mountains came down to celebrate.

Hither, also, came William Tell, and by his side walked his little son. He crossed the market-place. Those who saw him smiled at him and received in return the cordial greeting of a fellow patriot. He was, indeed, well loved and respected.

William Tell walked on, his little son's hand clasped in his own. He had a feeling of peace in his breast. And he sang a song of Swiss peasants—a joyous song!

Then he passed the Duke's hat on its long pole, with its feathers waving. But he did not bow, nor did he kneel.

Roughly was William Tell stopped by a guard. The song died on his lips.

He looked around to see the Governor beside him, surrounded by horsemen and guards.

"What is your name?" It was the gruff voice of Gessler himself.

"William Tell, the hunter, at your service, your honor," answered Tell.

"Ah, ah! William Tell! I know well who you are. And why did you not salute the hat?"

"Governor, I did not see it. I was not thinking."

"Um." The governor stroked his beard.

William Tell's little son began to cry.

The crowd pushed closer. Gessler bit his lip and thought.

"You are an archer, Tell?" he asked.

"Yes, your honor."

"Is that your son?"

"Yes, your honor."

"Have you others?"

"No, your honor. He is my only child."

"Good, good." The Governor stroked his beard once more. Then he went on, "William Tell, you have committed a great offence, but you do not seem to have done it knowingly. Therefore I shall give you only a light punishment."

So saying, the Governor took an apple from the basket of a peasant woman. Holding it up, he spoke again to William Tell.

"They say that you are renowned as an archer," he began, "that you shoot the chamois in its course, and birds on the wing. This apple shall be put upon the head of your son. You shall stand twenty paces away. If you hit the apple, your life will be granted you. But if you miss, your head will be cut off and will decorate the market-place as an example to others."

Tell did not speak, but the murmuring crowd could see that he trembled. Still silent, he chose an arrow, tried the point, and hid it in his blouse.

Then he selected another arrow and aimed. The little boy stood before him. The apple was poised on the

THE PAGEANT OF WILLIAM TELL

child's curly head. He was too frightened to move.

The renowned hunter trembles. Gessler smiles—a crooked smile. Tell aims a second time, and now his arm is steady. Through the air flies the arrow, and the apple falls, split in half. The crowd applauds, and the child runs to his father's arms. But Gessler is not satisfied.

"William Tell," said he, "I congratulate you. But tell me, why did you hide a second arrow in your blouse?"

Clutching his boy, the father answered the tyrant, "Because, had I killed my son, that arrow would have pierced your wicked heart!"

The Governor began to laugh.

"Well spoken, brave man," he said. "I gave you your life. But, as I still cherish my own, and you are too expert with the bow, you shall remain my prisoner for the rest of your life."

So saying, Gessler had William Tell bound, hand and foot, then took him away to the Governor's castle on an island.

The mountains looked down upon the scene and spoke, one to the other, "Hast witnessed this act of cruelty?"

"Yea," spoke the other, "and we shall take a hand in the situation."

The wind is the friend of the mountains, and the wind blew. A storm arose—a tempest on the lake! Green waves rose high, frothing white like mad dogs' lips. The waves boiled. The little boat rocked and shook like a leaf. The face of Gessler grew pale. His men could no longer row. The Governor could not swim.

At last one of his oarsmen said, "Tell is a splendid oarsman. He is the only one who can save us."

The frightened Governor cried to his captive, "Tell, if you will save us, I shall free you!"

In Tell's strong hands, the small bark was manned against the heavy storm, swiftly, skillfully. He rowed it toward the shore and a flat rock.

Then he felt in his blouse and touched the other arrow. His bow lay by his side. To the rock!

His arms pulled, and the boat flew across the angry waters. As it neared the shore, the hunter sprang upon the rock. Like a statue poised, he lifted his weapon, fitted the arrow, and shot. The wind died down. Later the little craft was found floating on the lake, face downward.

Once a year in a town of Switzerland, the peasants dress themselves in costumes and cover their faces with grease paint. Then some peasant turns actor, and the story of William Tell is dramatized.

A huge pageant is given in a lovely rural setting. It is more than a play. It is a rite. Thus the villagers honor their country's hero.

CHAPTER VII

MORE ABOUT SWITZERLAND

"In the village of Altdorf still stands the statue of that great man, William Tell. We visited the picturesque little town not long ago," said Mrs. Brownley, as Seppi drank in her words. "Then, too, we were fortunate in seeing the celebration of the Swiss National Festival on August first."

And she told of how she had seen the people in the towns dressed in the costumes of their cantons. The flags of the cantons were flying, along with their mother flag. This flag, with its

ALTDORF, THE HOME OF WILLIAM TELL

great red field and its white cross, floated above them all.

At eight o'clock at night, all the bells in the village rang, while a procession marched down the narrow streets. They had fireworks, music, and gymnastics (which the Swiss children call "gym." as we do).

They celebrate on the first of August in honor of an important event. Many years ago, three little cantons, Uri, Schwyz, and Unterwald became dissatisfied with the tyrannical rule of the Austrians. They were eager to obey their own cantonal masters. So they promised one another that, should trouble ever arise, they would always defend one another.

This declaration was signed on August 1, 1291, and exists to-day.

"You well know, Seppi, of the struggles which your little country has had, to defend itself and to live in peace," continued Mrs. Brownley. "Little by

SWISS CHILDREN MAKING LACE

little, the other cantons joined these three. This is how Switzerland gained her independence."

The Song Festival! "It is a real feast of music," said Mrs. Brownley, "for which the singers from all parts of Switzerland gather. In a large auditorium, they give a pageant of each canton.

"Thus hundreds of men, women and children raise their fresh, natural voices in praise of their country's beauty. The music they make as they perform their parts is indeed beautiful to hear.

"Lauterbrunnen is a lace town. From this mountain town comes some of the most beautiful lace in Switzerland.

"Old women, young girls, and children, some not more than five years old, sit at little tables outside the shops and work. Their fingers fly over the board on which they make

THE LION OF LUCERNE

the spidery lace. In this work they use many round-headed pins and little bobbins.

"Who has not heard of the 'Lion of Lucerne'? It stands on a massive rock, in a shaded park in the lovely city of Lucerne. It is carved out of the stone itself. It shows a suffering lion, dying from a wound in his side.

"This work of art marks the symbol of a battle fought in Paris in 1792. In this engagement, eight hundred soldiers of the Swiss Guard defended the Tuileries (tweel-re′) and lost their lives."

"Oh, please do not stop," said the boy, as Mrs. Brownley ceased. "Do tell me more."

"I have been in almost every part of your country, Seppi," continued the traveler. "I find it a playground —a country of pleasure, for the whole world to enjoy. But it is far from a pleasure-ground for the Swiss. The

LIFE IS HARD FOR THE SWISS PEASANT

peasants are a hard-working people. They are as industrious as the busy bee, which plies his trade without a moment's rest."

Seppi's eyes were raised to his

friend's, and his chin rested on his hand. Slowly he moved his position and shook his head sadly.

"Yes, you are right," he said. "We have little time for play. But we love to study. Although I went to school but a short time, I learned some things of interest, too, about my country. If you would like me to, I will tell you a legend which, perhaps, you have not heard."

"Oh, do," said Mrs. Brownley encouragingly. "I am so interested in all that pertains to your country! I am sure your story is interesting."

"Then please, dear lady, listen," said Seppi, "while I tell you the story of 'The Devil's Bridge'."

CHAPTER VIII
THE DEVIL'S BRIDGE

At the foot of the mountains, in the canton of Uri, flows the River Reuss, savage and bustling. Thousands of years ago, the population of Uri were anxious to have a stone bridge built to span the frothy river. It would also help to serve the growing traffic between Switzerland and Italy.

But in those olden times, the plan of building a stone bridge of such a size was too costly to be considered. For many days the people sat in long discussions.

After many useless talks, the

Mayor said, "Let us call in the Devil and consult with him."

At first the people were afraid to do this. For they knew how crafty the Devil is and were loath to lay themselves open to his trickery. But finally, all realized that it was the only way in which they might find an answer to their problem. So they agreed, and the Devil was called.

The Mayor explained to him that they wished a stone bridge. He asked how this could be done.

The Devil smiled cunningly and said, "I will build a bridge for you myself, and it will be a handsome one."

The people were delighted and told one another that they had surely been

THE DEVIL'S BRIDGE

mistaken in the Devil. For he was indeed kindly and generous.

Then up spoke the Devil again, his eyes gleaming, as he flicked his tail.

"But, good people, hearken," he said, "while I ask my reward for this labor. You surely did not expect me to do all this without some payment!"

The people became silent and grave and listened.

The Devil continued, "I have promised to build for you a fine stone bridge; and so I shall. But when it is finished, I demand that the first living being who crosses that bridge shall belong to me!"

The Mayor stroked his chin. Then the people began to whisper among themselves, and the Devil waited.

At last the Mayor spoke. "It shall be as you say," he told the Devil. "And when the bridge is finished, you shall claim the first living being that crosses it."

The Devil promised to complete the bridge the following day. Then with a flourish of his tail, he disappeared.

The next morning early when the people gathered, they found, to their amazement, a magnificent bridge of stone. Their joy, however, did not last long. For they noticed on the opposite side of the bridge the Devil, smiling and rubbing his hands. He was waiting for his pay.

"You have done your work well," said the Mayor to the Devil.

The Evil One sneered and thanked him for his praise.

Just then the Mayor caught a goat and pushed it upon the bridge. The goat, mistaking the Devil's horns for

the horns of a fellow goat, ran across
the bridge at him.

The Evil One saw how the Mayor
had deceived him and became a deep
red with fury. In a rage, he threw
the goat against the rocks. The
Mayor laughed. The people began to
see the joke that had been played
upon the Devil. They joined in the
mirth.

The deceived one, boiling with
rage, descended into the valley to
search for a huge rock. He intended
to use it to destroy the bridge he had
built. But as it was a long climb to
the top with the heavy rock, he rested
on the way up.

At this moment, an old woman

passed. Seeing the Devil with his large rock, she thought that he was about to do something wicked. Good Christian that she was, she made the sign of the cross with her hand first upon herself and then toward the rock.

The Devil tried once more to lift the rock but did not succeed. Looking up, he saw the good woman making the sign of the cross over and over again.

This sign completely destroyed his powers. He fled to the lower regions whence he had come. He left behind him the rock and the beautiful bridge, unharmed. And that is why it is still called "The Devil's Bridge."

CHAPTER IX

SEPPI'S CARVING

"What a strange story! I had never heard that before," said the lady.

"But Seppi," she continued, "we are forgetting why you have come. Surely your father sent my carving?"

Dazed, Seppi nodded and tried to smile.

Pulling his own little dog out of his pouch, he handed it tremblingly to the lady. His eyes did not leave Mrs. Brownley's face. She took the carving from him with intense interest.

She was expecting something beautiful. She had told his father that he was an artist. She had ordered the little work only because she believed in the old man's skill.

Now she would see this poor little copy! Oh, the ear was crooked! Seppi had never noticed that before. It was surely crooked. And it was not smooth—not smooth. It swam there before him. It became soft like putty. It—

A hand came down gently on his shoulder, and a voice said, "Why, Seppi, this is even lovelier than I had expected it to be. And I had really looked forward to something very fine! But your father is a greater genius than I had thought."

It seemed to Seppi that the whole

world had stopped turning. Every
moment of his life seemed to come
running up to meet this moment.
The tall lady standing before him
seemed like a goddess pronouncing
his fate. And that fate was sweet.

It dawned on the slow peasant boy
that his work—his own untaught
work—was being given the praise due
his father's—the master's! Then it
all became clear to his poor, muddled
brain. A stab went through him.

"I have deceived!" he thought.

Mrs. Brownley laid the dog gently
on the table with her other posses-
sions. Then she picked up her purse.

"Here, Seppi," she said. "Take this
money to your father. Tell him that

SOON HE CAME TO THE SAME SHRINE

this little dog which he has carved is my dearest and most valuable treasure!"

Seppi could never remember just how he left Mrs. Brownley or what he said. His brain was whirling about.

Soon he came to the same shrine where his basket had been stolen.

It seemed a year since he had stood on that spot and watched those two boys running down the path with his father's carving.

He fell on his knees. A prayer flowed from his lips. His troubled face was raised to the kindly wooden Virgin above him.

The clouds gathered around the Wetterhorn, while that haughty mountain raised his head above them. He seemed to be stretching his neck in order not to miss that sight of the little goat-boy praying.

"Oh, God, please forgive me for deceiving!" prayed Seppi.

"FORGIVE ME FOR DECEIVING!"

He thought of the little cabin standing alone and guarded by the mountains. An old man was waiting inside, with a look of questioning. Seppi seemed to see himself telling Joseph of his success.

"But, oh, thank thee, dear God, for helping me. Thank thee, thank thee!" So ran his prayer.

The Wetterhorn shrank down below the clouds. Perhaps he had seen enough. Perhaps, tall, strong guardian that he is, did not want to show his feelings.

CHAPTER X

ALONE

It was just a year since Seppi had come home that evening and poured the money, given him by Mrs. Brownley, into the eager hands of his old father. It was just a year since the man and the boy had sat outside their little Swiss home, talking about the experiences of the day.

Seppi had just told his father all that had happened. How thrilled Seppi had been to show his father the little works his hands had carved on the mountain!

They were all little copies of Jo-

"YOU WILL BE A GREAT CARVER, MY SON!"

seph's works. Each one was better than the last.

"Ah, Seppi," Joseph had said proudly, "my son, you are a great artist!"

Then the old wood-carver sat very

still for a few moments. He was thinking just what to say to his son.

At last he said, "Seppi, we cannot keep the money you have brought from Mrs. Brownley. The work you delivered to her may be as good or better than mine, but it was a copy of the work she should have received. We must not make a sale in this manner.

"Early in the morning, take the money, go to Mrs. Brownley, and tell her exactly what happened. Apologize, and offer to return the money to her, and to take back the carving. If, after you have done this, she still desires to keep the work, and wishes you to retain the money, you may do so.

This will make everything right."

Early the next morning Seppi went to Grindelwald to return the money to Mrs. Brownley. But when he arrived there Mrs. Brownley was gone —gone to America. There was nothing more Seppi could do to correct his error. He, therefore, returned to his father with a heavy heart.

Joseph said, "Mrs. Brownley will probably come back next year. We will put the money away and keep it for her until she returns.

"I will make another carving, the same as the first. When Mrs. Brownley returns she may then take the carving or the money, either one she desires."

"MAY I REALLY GO TO SCHOOL IN BRIENZ, FATHER?"

Again Joseph talked of Seppi's carvings. He was very much pleased with the work his son had done.

He said, "You shall go to the school at Brienz, my son, and learn. I shall send you next winter."

How the boy danced with joy at these words! Next winter!

Then next winter had come and with it such a change!

For now, just a year since all this had taken place, Seppi was alone. Alone and without Joseph! At the first signs of winter, the old man had left his son. Joseph was dead.

Seppi, now taller and manlier, lived by himself in the cabin. All thoughts of school and study were gone. All golden plans and hopes were destroyed.

For many months the poor boy had sorrowed alone. His daily goat duty had kept him busy, but his heart yearned for the dear companion. He longed for the jolly, wrinkled face which had lit up each evening when he came home. He yearned to hear the hearty voice that had followed him up the mountain side every morning.

Those were lonely days.

But one evening, as Seppi was seated at his solitary meal, a shop-keeper from the village arrived.

"Ah, Seppi," he called. "We do not see you in the town any more. Why do you not come?"

Seppi bade the man be seated and join him in his repast.

"The village is far away," he said, "and I have little time to go there."

"But Seppi," continued the man,

"our shop misses your father's works. We wonder why you do not bring some in to sell. We know that Joseph kept many carvings here, which he made throughout the winter and did not sell. We can use these, Seppi, and will buy them from you."

Now Seppi had often thought of taking to the shop these works which his father had left. He had this thought whenever poverty pinched sorely.

But always, as he had about made up his mind to do so, something would stop him.

Those fine, little carved animals were the only companions he had. He had learned to love them like live things. Then, too, they were his only souvenirs of his father.

"Yes. Father left many beautiful works," replied the boy. "But I could never bring myself to part with them."

"Ah, come, Seppi," urged the shop-keeper. "They will bring good money. This will be a prosperous season, and we can sell them all."

Seppi sighed and said, "Perhaps I shall come with them some day, but not yet. I must think."

Shaking his puzzled head, the man bade Seppi good night and left.

For many days, Seppi thought over the shopkeeper's offer. How happy poor Joseph would have been, could he but be here now to work for this busy tourist season!

And then, one day, Seppi was sitting on his rock, with the goats about him, and his knife busy in his hand. For Seppi always carved on the mountain side, though his works usually remained unfinished.

Suddenly as he sat and carved, a thought came to him.

He said to himself, "Father would have been pleased." He kept repeating this over and over. That night he gathered his father's animals about him and spoke to them as to children.

"Now you shall never leave me!" he cried. "I have a plan. I shall copy you. I shall sell you but keep you!"

Seppi laughed at his own words. For the first time in many months, he was happy.

Then began a period of joyous labor for the lad. He took all his father's animals to the mountains with him and copied them.

He made a brother for each animal. And that brother, much to the young carver's delight, was exactly like his mate. In fact, it was only Seppi himself who could have told them apart.

When they were all finished, he made a trip to the village below. To the shop he went and presented the little figures.

"Ah, you have decided to sell them, then, Seppi!" laughed the shopkeeper.

"You will not be sorry. You will see the money they bring."

Then upon examining the works, he added, "What beauty! These last ones seem to be better than any before. There is no other carver like Joseph! Are there more of these, my lad? If there are, we can sell them all!"

"Yes," he answered. "I can supply you with carvings of this kind for many months."

The shopkeeper smiled, "Ah, that is a fine bit of news! Bring them to me; but not all at once. For I cannot sell them so quickly, you know. A few at a time."

"I will bring you only a few at a time," said Seppi.

Then Seppi told the shopkeeper that he had carved these animals himself. They were copies of his father's carvings.

He said, "I will not sell my father's works, but, if you wish to purchase mine, I will furnish you as many as you desire."

The shopkeeper was so surprised he could not speak for a few moments. He first looked at Seppi, and then at the animals, as if he could hardly believe what he had heard.

Then he took Seppi by the hand and said, "Seppi, you will be a greater artist than your father. I will buy your carvings, and will pay you well for them. I know they will sell. They will surely be admired as much as those your father made."

Seppi could hardly thank the shop-keeper enough for his kind words, and for his generous offer to purchase his carvings. After promising to return soon with more animals, he started home. He seemed to be lifted up from the ground—just walking on air.

The first thing he did when he entered his little home was to take Joseph's carvings from the cupboard. He spread them out upon the table.

Then he cried, "Now, I shall keep you always, and they may think that mine are as good as you. But I know better! You are the dearest things in the world to me!"

CHAPTER XI
THE LITTLE WOOD-CARVER

One day the sky was so blue and the mountains were so clear that it seemed they had edged up closer. They seemed about to pounce upon the little village of Grindelwald. On this day, a lady climbed the steep hills and looked about her for a familiar sign.

It was Mrs. Brownley coming again to her favorite Switzerland. She was just as interested as on the day she had first attracted the attention of Seppi, when she had attempted to climb the Jungfrau. She was again

THE LITTLE SWISS WOOD-CARVER

on her way to the home of the goat-boy.

She could not remember the exact spot where the wood-carver dwelt. So she was puzzled. But as she wandered on, she soon saw a curling line of smoke rising from between two mountains. Knowing that this meant a cabin, she pushed on, in the hope that she would find the one she sought.

As Mrs. Brownley drew nearer, she could see Seppi's house from where she stood. It made a sweet picture, with its little, slanting roof, upon which lay many stones. They had been put there, as on all Alpine roofs, to hold the roof down.

For there were many severe summer blasts which might well lift and carry the little roof away, when the snow of winter is not there to hold it down.

The cabin stood as it had stood on that day when she had first seen Joseph's art treasures. On that day she had ordered her little carving.

She had come back now to order more. She also wished to chat once again with the boy, whom she had never forgotten.

As she looked, she saw an unusual figure sitting before the cabin at Joseph's work table. It was not Joseph, the carver, but her little friend Seppi.

Like most Alpine climbers, Mrs.

Brownley carried glasses with which to look far into the mountains. Now she leveled these at the sight before her. As she focused her glass, a strange surprise greeted her.

Through the glasses appeared the goat-boy of former days. He was now a lad, large and strong and manly, working with deft hands at a most beautiful carving.

The work was large, and she could see it clearly. It represented a mare with her colt by her side, its baby nose nestling along her sleek body. The two figures were in motion. Moreover, the grace of that pair delighted Mrs. Brownley.

Her feet became rooted to the spot.

She did not move until the boy, weary with his labors, stopped his carving.

He stretched his arms above his head and leaned back in his chair. Then Mrs. Brownley put away her glasses and hurried forward. . . . . . .

"Seppi, lunch is ready!"

Seppi opened his sleepy eyes and looked about him.

"I say, lunch is ready, Seppi. Come!"

It was a woman's voice, and it came from the porch.

Seppi arose, taking with him the precious carving of the mare and colt. He rounded the corner of the house.

There, seated beside the little stove, was his friend Mrs. Brownley! She was stirring the steaming soup and smiling up at him.

Seppi could hardly believe his eyes.

He stammered, "But lady, you—"

Then he realized that he held the carving in his hands. With a quick motion, he tried to hide it behind his back.

"Do not hide that, Seppi," she said. "Let me see it."

She put out her hands, and Seppi was forced to show her his unfinished work.

"And so you, too, have become a carver," she said, "and such a clever one! This is a work of art, my boy."

Then while they ate in front of the crude little stove, Seppi told Mrs.

Brownley of his troubled, sorrowful times.

He explained how he had been copying his father's works and selling them to the village store.

"I could not part with my father's works," he said. "They are so dear to me; so I copied them."

Then the boy related his sad experiences of that day when he delivered to Mrs. Brownley the carving of the St. Bernard dog. He ended his story by asking Mrs. Brownley to forgive him, and offering her the return of the money or the second carving his father had made.

Mrs. Brownley was so quiet, when he had finished, that he feared she must be angry. But she took his hand gently in hers.

"Seppi," she said, "you have my forgiveness without the asking. I could not think of taking either the money or the carving. I much prefer to keep the carving you made.

Then Mrs. Brownley said, "Seppi, you must not stay here. You are a great carver. You are as great as, if not greater than, your father was. I am going to see that you are sent to another part of Switzerland for a few years. There you will learn another language and finish your education.

"Then you shall carve, Seppi, carve! And your works will always be sold, for you shall send them to America to my husband's big shop. What do you say, Seppi?"

At first Seppi could not believe what he heard. Was his dream really to come true? After this year of disappointment and grief, would Joseph's promise be at last fulfilled?

"You shall go to study and become a master, my son!" Joseph had said.

The words rang in his ears!

"And may I go to Brienz and study?" he asked simply.

Mrs. Brownley smiled a bit sadly, as she struggled to keep back the words, "You are greater than those who would teach you there!"

But she only thought this and said aloud, "Yes, Seppi, if you care to.

INTERNATIONAL LABOR OFFICE, GENEVA

But first you must learn in school the things that other children have been learning while you tended your goats."

Seppi fell on his knees and kissed the lady's hand, over and over again.

All that day they sat and talked together.

He showed her the lovely pieces he had carved. Then evening came.

His friend said, "I must go now, Seppi. But to-morrow I will return with my husband, and we will take you with us to Geneva. We know a family there, with whom you shall live while you learn to speak French and finish your education."

"I shall be ready to go," said the boy. "And oh, thank you, thank you, kind lady!"

"Then, good-bye until to-morrow, my little Swiss wood-carver!" she said.

And she was gone.

CHAPTER XII
GOOD-BYE TO HIS HOME

"Good-bye, my mountains. Good-bye, my goats. Good-bye, my little wooden cabin!" cried Seppi.

He stood on the edge of the mountain and gazed in dim-eyed affection upon the scene of his whole life.

It was morning, and he was awaiting Mrs. Brownley's arrival. Wrapped up in his bundle were his working clothes. He was wearing his velvet costume, with the gold braid glistening in the morning sunshine.

Beside the bundle of clothing was another bundle—a bulkier bundle, a more precious bundle. It contained his father's carvings.

"But though I leave you all behind, my home, my mountains, my goats, I take my dearest with me! My father's carvings!" he whispered.

As he glanced below, he saw the figures of his friends coming upward. He slung his two bundles upon his shoulders. Then with a song on his lips, he wended his way down the mountain toward a new life.